A Beginning-to-Read Book

Dear Dragon Goes to the Carnival

by Margaret Hillert

Illustrated by David Schimmell

NORWOOD HOUSE PRESS

DEAR CAREGIVER, The *Beginning-to-Read* series is a carefully written collection of classic readers you may remember from your own childhood. Each book features text comprised of common sight words to provide your child ample practice reading the words that appear most frequently in written text. The many additional details in the pictures enhance the story and offer the opportunity for you to help your child expand oral language and develop comprehension.

Begin by reading the story to your child, followed by letting him or her read familiar words and soon your child will be able to read the story independently. At each step of the way, be sure to praise your reader's efforts to build his or her confidence as an independent reader. Discuss the pictures and encourage your child to make connections between the story and his or her own life. At the end of the story, you will find reading activities and a word list that will help your child practice and strengthen beginning reading skills.

Above all, the most important part of the reading experience is to have fun and enjoy it!

Shannon Cannon

Shannon Cannon,
Literacy Consultant

Norwood House Press • P.O. Box 316598 • Chicago, Illinois 60631
For more information about Norwood House Press please visit our website at
www.norwoodhousepress.com or call 866-565-2900.

LIBRARY OF CONGRESS CATALOGING-IN-PUBLICATION DATA

Hillert, Margaret.
   Dear dragon goes to the carnival / by Margaret Hillert ; illustrated by David Schimmell.
    p. cm. -- (A beginning-to-read book)
   Summary: "A boy and his pet dragon spend a day at the carnival going on
rides and playing different games"--Provided by publisher.
    ISBN-13: 978-1-59953-346-9 (library edition : alk. paper)
    ISBN-10: 1-59953-346-4 (library edition : alk. paper)
   [1. Dragons--Fiction. 2. Carnivals--Fiction.] I. Schimmell, David, ill. II. Title.
PZ7.H558Dee 2010
[E]--dc22

                      2009031728

Manufactured in the United States of America in North Mankato, Minnesota.
160N—072010

Can we go?
Can we go, Mother?
It will be fun, fun, fun.

Can you go where?
Where do you want to go?

There is a spot
where you can ride,
you can play,
and you can eat something.

Oh, that spot.
I guess so.
Father will want to come, too.

Oh, boy!
Good, good, good.
We can all have fun.

7

We can go now.
Get in the car.
Get in. Get in.
Away we go.

There it is!
There it is!
Oh, look at it!

I want to go on this.
I like this ride.
It looks like fun.

Go, go, go.
Away, away, away.
Oh, it is fun!

Can we go on
this one, Father?
Will you go with me?

Here we go.
Up, up, up.

Oh, look down there.
Way, way down.
I can see Mother.
Mother looks little.

Oh, Mother. We were way up.
We saw you. We saw you down here.
You were little.

I saw you, too.
Way up there.

But look at this.
See the red, yellow, and blue balls.
This is a good game.

Father, can you do this?
Can you make three balls go in?
Can you get me something?

Oh, you did it!
You did it!
Look what I have.
A funny, good friend.

We can get something here.
What do you want?
What do you like?

This is what I like.
Mmmmmmmmmmm.
This apple is so good.

We have to go now.
Are you happy?
Was it fun?

27

Yes, yes Mother.
Fun, fun, fun.

Here you are with me.
And here I am with you.
What a happy, happy day, dear dragon.

The following activities support the findings of the National Reading Panel that determined the most effective components for reading instruction are: Phonemic Awareness, Phonics, Vocabulary, Fluency, and Text Comprehension.

Phonemic Awareness: The /n/ sound

Sound Substitution: Say the following words to your child and ask him or her to substitute the first sound in the word with /**n**/:

tap = nap	seed = need	fear = near
peck = neck	mice = nice	best = nest
fight = night	zip = nip	hose = nose
how = now	fine = nine	game = name
wet = net	kick = nick	

Phonics: The letters N and n

1. Demonstrate how to form the letters **N** and **n** for your child.

2. Have your child practice writing **N** and **n** at least three times each.

3. Write down the following words and ask your child to circle the letter **n** in each word:

and	fun	can	down	now
then	something	want	carnival	net
clown	grin	song	balloon	noon
run	nut	ring		

Vocabulary: Making Words

1. Write the words **the carnival** at the top of a piece of paper.

2. Write each letter in the words **the carnival** on separate small pieces of paper.

3. Explain to your child that the letters in the words **the** and **carnival** can be used to make new words.

4. Provide the following clues and help your child use the letters to make the correct words. Ask your child to write the words on the paper under **the carnival**.

- Something you drive. (car)
- The number that comes between nine and eleven. (ten)
- Something you carry things in, like groceries at the store. (cart)
- The name for a female chicken. (hen)
- A monkey can use this to hang from trees. (tail)
- The rubber part of a wheel on a car or truck. (tire)
- Another word for skinny. (thin)
- Something you can sit on. (chair)
- The part of the body that goes with love. (heart)
- You go to school to do this. (learn)

Fluency: Shared Reading

1. Reread the story with your child at least two more times while your child tracks the print by running a finger under the words as they are read. Ask your child to read the words he or she knows with you.

2. Reread the story taking turns, alternating readers between sentences or pages.

Text Comprehension: Discussion Time

1. Ask your child to retell the sequence of events in the story.

2. To check comprehension, ask your child the following questions:
- What rides did the boy go on at the carnival?
- Why did the boy say his mother looked little?
- Why did the clown give the boy a bear?
- What is your favorite part of this carnival? Why?

***Dear Dragon Goes to the Carnival* uses the 77 words listed below**. This list can be used to practice reading the words that appear in the text. You may wish to write the words on index cards and use them to help your child build automatic word recognition. Regular practice with these words will enhance your child's fluency in reading connected text.

a	day	happy	oh	three
all	dear	have	on	to
am	did	here	one	too
and	do			
apple	down	I	play	up
are	dragon	in		
at		is	red	want
away	eat	it	ride	was
				way
balls	Father	like	saw	we
be	friend	little	see	were
blue	fun	look(s)	so	what
boy	funny		something	where
but		make	spot	will
	game	me		with
can	get	Mother	that	
car	go		the	yellow
come	good	now	there	yes
	guess		this	you

ABOUT THE AUTHOR Margaret Hillert has written over 80 books for children who are just learning to read. Her books have been translated into many different languages and over a million children throughout the world have read her books. She first started writing poetry as a child and has continued to write for children and adults throughout her life. A first grade teacher for 34 years, Margaret is now retired from teaching and lives in Michigan where she likes to write, take walks in the morning, and care for her three cats.

Photograph by Glenna Washburn

ABOUT THE ADVISER Shannon Cannon contributed the activities pages that appear in this book. Shannon serves as a literacy consultant and provides staff development to help improve reading instruction. She is a frequent presenter at educational conferences and workshops. Prior to this she worked as an elementary school teacher and as president of a curriculum publishing company.